Simo
Boug

The Manor House Stories

Somewhere deep in the heart of the English countryside, many years ago, stood a large Manor House. In the House lived a family of birds. Upstairs and downstairs all the birds played their part in looking after it. In the gardens, the village and on the farm, the birds and animals worked together, in harmony with nature, to preserve the traditions and idyllic way of life that have disappeared long ago.

The Manor House Stories follow the adventures of the characters and their duties, from the lowliest scullery maid upwards through the ranks of the household to the head of the family. From time to time surprising visitors arrive at the House; from a princess to a pirate, you never know who may appear to cast their magic and mischief over the Manor House...

**written and illustrated
by Jani Tully Chaplin**

The Manor House Stories are a series of twelve small books for children that Jani wrote and illustrated, based on her observations and inspirations while raising her two children, Rory and Miranda, at their family home in the heart of the Devonshire countryside.

Cream & Sugar the Milkmaids | Snowfall and Snowballs The first snow has fallen, and the youngsters have fun in the garden. A mysterious visitor arrives in a beautiful sleigh. Erminetine the Stoat makes an ice sculpture and is rewarded with a special gift.

Rory Redshank the Footman | The Prince's Visit The Prince's visit causes a stir. Rory has an accident with the red carpet, and Delia Duck the Cook makes heart shaped biscuits as a gift to the Prince for St. Valentine's Day.

Sarah Sparrow the Scullery Maid | A Fine Romance Sarah meets Jeremy Jackdaw the Chimneysweep. Romance blossoms and before long the Manor House is hoping for a spring wedding.

Patience Pigeon the Nanny | The New Arrival Easter celebrations abound at the Manor House with an Easter egg hunt and the exciting arrival of the new baby. Patience has an accident at the pond. Can anyone save the baby?

Miss Miranda Mistlethrush | The Birthday Party Lady Davina Dove and Lord Peregrine Falcon's daughter, Miranda, spends hours in the bathroom. On her 13th birthday a party is held in the garden. Granny and Grandpa McGrouse bring a surprise guest.

Tilly Titmouse the Parlourmaid | The Broken Vase Tilly breaks a vase and asks for Safari Swallow's help to mend it. Meg Magpie the Gypsy appears with her caravan and tells Tilly's fortune by looking into a crystal ball.

Chesterfield Penguin the Butler | All at Sea The Manor House family makes a trip to the seaside. The twins, Arthur and Sebastian, launch their raft. Blown out to sea they call for help. Sailor Oswald Seagull and Chesterfield Penguin are their only hope.

Radish Robin the Gardener | The Harvest Home Delia Duck makes strawberry jam. The twins 'help' Radish decorate the barn for the Harvest Home. Pieces of Eight the Pirate appears and is caught with his beak in the jam. A surprise awaits the twins, Arthur and Sebastian.

Sgt. Simon Squirrel the Quartermaster | The Battle of the Squirrels The Manor House Stores are under attack by the Grey Squirrel Gang. Sgt. Simon enlists help from his ex-army chums, the red squirrels and Octavius Owl the wise old schoolmaster.

Ottermere Otter the Water Bailiff | The Great Flood The Manor House is in danger of flooding. Ottermere Otter enlists the help of Barkus Beaver the Carpenter who diverts the river. Wartella Peckster the Hairy Woodpecker conjures up an evil plan for Bonfire Night.

Masters Arthur & Sebastian | The Bonfire Party The twins prepare for a Bonfire Night party. Miranda makes Yum Yum Choc Chips (recipe included.) A scary time is had in the dark woods, when Wartella Peckster the Witch takes her revenge. Arthur and Sebastian learn an important lesson.

Lady Davina Dove | A Christmas Story Christmas has come to the Manor House. Everyone is busy preparing for the merrymaking. Stockings are hung, the Christmas tree is decorated, and Father Christmas arrives by moonlight. On Christmas Day Lady Davina's secret wish comes true.

First published in the United Kingdom in 2013
by **Mark Hendriksen Publishing**
copyright © 2013 Jani Tully Chaplin | Mark Hendriksen

ISBN 978-0-9565443-2-2

Edit & Design: Mark Hendriksen, Chris Johnson, Lara Fisher | Design: Davor Delija

www.themanorhousestories.co.uk

Printed & bound in the UK by Cambrian Printers

A catalogue record for this title is available from The British Library. The publisher's policy is to print using papers that are both natural and renewable. The FSC accreditation guarantees that the paper came from a sustainably managed forest.

FSC
www.fsc.org
MIX
Paper from
responsible sources
FSC® C005094

Foreword by Julian Fellowes

The Manor House Stories create a wonderful and detailed world in miniature full of truth and consequence, like all good stories should, giving us lessons about life but in the most charming way imaginable. No one can accuse the books of soft-soaping the realities of work in a great house; there is plenty of elbow grease required from all the animals and birds employed there, as I should know, but you will find kindness in these pages too, and I suppose I believe that while fate may be challenging for everyone, there is often some kindness in the mix. In my experience anyway.

These lovely little tales contain comments and observations that will be very useful to young readers in the years to come, and they will be useful to older readers too, if I am anything to go by.

Julian Fellowes

This book belongs to...

draw yourself as a character here

Lady Davina Dove

Lord Peregrine Falcon

Patience Pigeon the Nanny

Lady Davina Dove

Miss Miranda Mistlethrush

Arthur and Sebastian the Twins

George the Baby Duckling

Sir David Bunnyburrow

Chesterfield Penquin the Butler

Sgt. Simon Squirrel the Quartermaster

Meet the Characters...

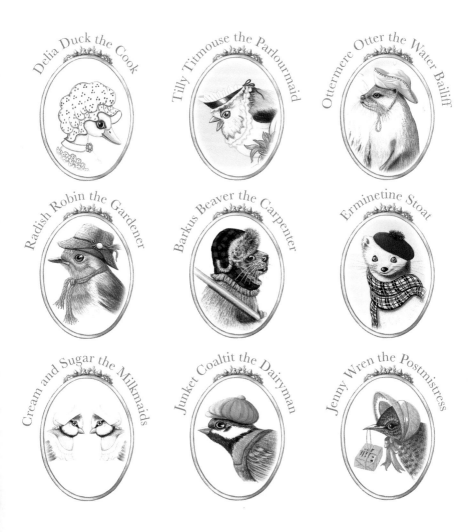

Delia Duck the Cook

Tilly Titmouse the Parlourmaid

Ottermere Otter the Water Bailiff

Radish Robin the Gardener

Barkus Beaver the Carpenter

Erminetine Stoat

Cream and Sugar the Milkmaids

Junket Coaltit the Dairyman

Jenny Wren the Postmistress

Lady Davina Dove

A CHRISTMAS STORY

It was the morning of Christmas Eve. The youngsters of the Manor House, Miranda Mistlethrush and the Willow Tit twins, Arthur and Sebastian, were bursting with excitement.

Indeed, everyone was looking forward to Christmas Day. There would be parties and feasts, singing and dancing, decorations and games.

Lady Davina had been busy shopping. There were such a lot of presents to buy.

But Lady Davina still had one particular wish for herself, for a very special Christmas present that she had wanted ever since she could remember. So far that wish had never ever come true.

As usual Lord Peregrine had left all the organising of the household to Lady Davina, who in turn gave Chesterfield Penguin the Butler her long list of instructions.

This year Lord Peregrine had invited Sir David Bunnyburrow to stay for Christmas. Sir David was his oldest friend, who knew nearly everything about nature and his fellow birds and animals.

He was eagerly awaiting his friend's arrival and the opportunity to chat about ways to protect any creatures that might be suffering during the cold and wet winter months.

Meanwhile, over at the dairy, Cream and Sugar the Milkmaids were twittering with excitement. From the moment they woke up they had been wondering how they would ever be able to sleep a single wink that night.

Junket the Dairyman had promised they could take Christmas Day off, as long as they delivered the clotted cream, milk and cheese to Delia Duck the Cook first thing on Christmas morning.

Cream and Sugar did not mind at all, for they knew that Delia would give them a Christmas present of hot mince pies, as she did every year. Imagining the delicious pies they quickly set to work.

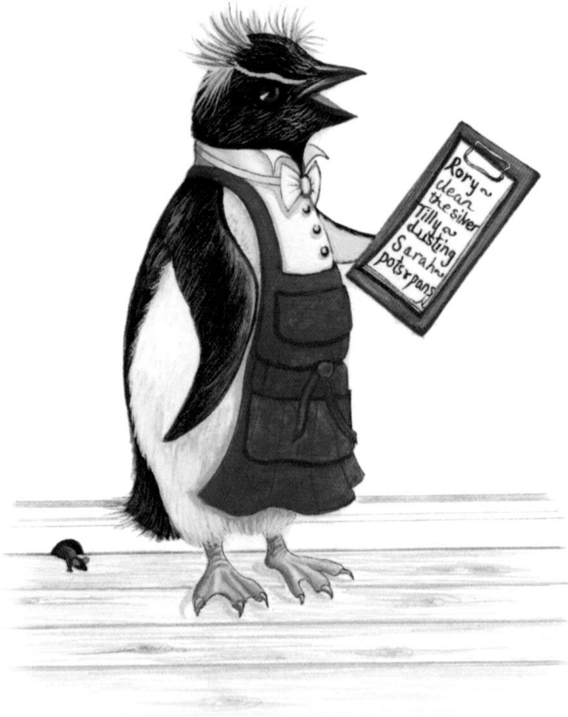
Rory ~
clean
the silver
Tilly ~
dusting
Sarah ~
pots & pans

Chesterfield Penguin the Butler was in a rare frenzy as he ticked off each item on Lady Davina's list. It was up to him to make sure all his staff did their best to prepare the House for the festivities.

He told Rory Redshank the Footman to clean the silver, and asked Tilly Titmouse the Parlourmaid to dust everything. Sarah Sparrow the Scullery Maid had the hardest jobs of all: scrubbing floors, laying fires and then cleaning all the brass pots and pans until she was able see her face in them.

In the nursery, Patience Pigeon the Nanny had her wings full too.

Not only did she have to keep the twins under control, which was nearly impossible as they were full of mischief at all times, but this particular Christmas she also had the newest member of the Manor House nursery to look after. Little George was still only eight months old.

Patience preferred to call him Pitter-Patter, a pet name that suited his rather large feet.

Luckily for Patience, Miranda was a great help, as she adored her little brother. She spent hours tidying the nursery, arranging the toys, and making sure the tiny clothes were folded neatly. Then she would sing to George as he fell asleep in his cot.

Miranda's favourite job was giving George his bath. He loved splashing about in the water and always tried to catch the hundreds of bubbles with his beak.

All the while, Delia Duck was busy in the kitchen. Starting early in December she had been making mince pies, Christmas pudding, Christmas cake and star-shaped biscuits flavoured with cinnamon, as well as the other favourite dishes of the household.

Radish Robin the Gardener brought fresh vegetables, including Brussels sprouts, which the twins had refused to eat last Christmas, even when they were told they could not have any pudding if they left them!

Delia received most of her ingredients from Sgt. Simon Squirrel the Quartermaster, who had been storing hoards of nuts, berries, apples and seeds in his storeroom in the big hollow tree since the autumn.

He brought Delia chestnuts for roasting, dried mushrooms and some of her jars of chutney and crab apple jelly that he had been keeping for Christmas.

If Sgt. Simon and the Manor Guard had not saved the stores from the attack by the Grey Squirrel Gang in September, there would simply not have been enough food to go around.

Jenny Wren the Postmistress had been visiting the
Manor House every morning, busily delivering
Christmas cards and interesting looking parcels
tied up with brown paper and string.

Christmas was Jenny's favourite time of year. She liked collecting stamps from different countries and today, as it was Christmas Eve, this would be her last delivery until the New Year.

Jenny delivered a card from the youngsters' favourite uncle, the Australian Ambassador Sir Prize Cockatoo. She asked to keep the stamp, which showed a kangaroo with a green and gold festive garland on its head.

Barkus Beaver the Carpenter and Radish Robin the Gardener had planted a whole forest of fir trees, so there would always be one special tree for the House at Christmas.

Barkus had found the perfect tree and brought it back to the Manor. He had been keeping his beady eyes on it for a few years now, waiting for it to grow big enough to reach the ceiling in the hall. Barkus then went off to find Ottermere Otter the Water Bailiff.

"Ahoy there Ottermere!" he called as he reached Brooke Lodge, the houseboat where Ottermere lived. "I've brought you an early Christmas present."

He handed Ottermere a tiny fir tree in a pot. "It's growing in this pot of earth, so we can plant it just after Christmas. You must remember to water it though."

Ottermere smiled. This was an easy job for him, because the only thing he liked as much as food, and fish in particular, was water.

Erminetine Stoat, who was in charge of the ice house, made her way through the quiet woods from her cold underground home wearing her white winter coat. She also wore gloves to protect her paws, and boots that she had been given by a Russian princess who had visited the Manor House earlier that year.

Today she was taking a supply of her precious ice to Delia Duck, who was making special blackberry ice cream. Sgt. Simon had carefully dried the berries and stored them since August, when Miranda and the twins had gingerly plucked them from the prickly brambles.

As soon as the tree was in place in the hall, Lady Davina, Miranda and the twins began to pick the Christmas decorations out of a wicker basket, which had been brought down from the attic.

"Please can I put the star on the top?" asked Arthur.

"No, please let me," said Sebastian. "I'm the oldest twin!"

"Only by five minutes!" protested Arthur.

When the tree was decorated, Lord Peregrine was persuaded to leave his study to admire all their handiwork; then, as head of the family, he carefully lit the first candle. The family all clapped and cheered with joy.

(As there was no electricity in those days at the House, small candles in metal holders were clipped onto the branches of the Christmas tree.)

Lady Davina had neatly arranged all the presents for everyone under the tree. She had to shoo the twins away, as they were trying to prod all the parcels and guess what was inside.

"Come on, you two," Miranda said. "It's time to go carol singing."

"Yippee!" shouted the twins together, flying off to put on their hats and warm scarves.

Miranda took a lantern, and they headed out towards the village.

Cream and Sugar joined them, twittering excitedly as they hurried along. Their first stop was at the Post Office where Jenny Wren lived.

They began to sing:

"The holly and the ivy,
When they are both full grown,
Of all the trees that are in the wood,
The holly bears the crown."

"Oh, the rising of the sun and the running of the deer," warbled a sweet voice from the upstairs window.

It was Jenny Wren, who was well known for her beautiful song and could be heard singing early each morning as she delivered the post.

Jenny came to the
front door.
"Thank you so much, my
dears," Jenny said. "Here's
a little something for you."

She handed Miranda
a paper bag full of
crystallised cranberries
that she had made herself
and said, "A very Merry
Christmas to you all."

It was getting rather late by the time the little group had sung to every cottage in the village. The night frost was already glittering in the light of the lantern.

Cream and Sugar hurried off to their snug loft above the dairy, and the others were equally glad to get back to the warmth and cosiness of the Manor House.

 36

Chesterfield was waiting for them in the hall, with steaming mugs of hot chocolate on a silver tray.

"I thought you might need something to warm you up," he said with a kindly smile.

The chocolate was delicious and had a thick topping of whipped cream. The twins looked very funny as the cream left tiny white moustaches above their beaks!

Upstairs in the nursery Tilly Titmouse the Parlourmaid, who had been patiently waiting until Christmas Eve, was finally able to hang the family's stockings from the mantelpiece above the fireplace.

Downstairs in the drawing room, Miranda and the twins left a plate of Delia's delicious shortbread biscuits and a glass of sherry next to the hearth for Father Christmas, and of course, a large carrot for his favourite reindeer, Rudolph.

(Yes, the one with the red nose, although it was in danger of turning bright orange from eating so many carrots!)

"When will Father Christmas fill our stockings?" asked Arthur.

"Not until you are both fast asleep!" said Lady Davina, leading the twins upstairs to the nursery.

Every Christmas Eve, once they were tucked up in their bed, she recited the same poem, as it always seemed to make them sleepy.

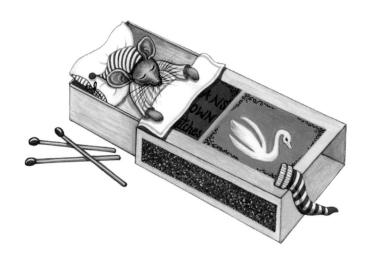

"Twas the night before Christmas,
When all through the house,
Not a creature was stirring,
Not even a mouse.
The stockings were hung by the
chimney with care..."

And sure enough, they closed their eyes
and both drifted off to sleep.

Lord Peregrine's guest, Sir David Bunnyburrow, had arrived a short while earlier and joined Lord Peregrine in the study. They were deep in conversation about the fate that had almost left many of the creatures homeless just a couple of months earlier.

"After Ottermere saved the Manor House from the Great Flood last October, we needed to replace all the damaged trees that Farmer Couldntcareless had cut down in Lookweep meadows," said Lord Peregrine.

"Of course you did!" replied Sir David. Without trees and hedges where would all the small animals and birds find a safe place to live?"

"Luckily we were able to replant the chestnut
and oak saplings that had sprouted around the
Oak Tree Storeroom, where all the acorns and
conkers fell on the ground during the Battle
of the Squirrels in September," explained
Lord Peregrine.

"Good for you!" said Sir David cheerfully.

"Apart from planting new trees, I also asked Barkus and Radish to repair our hedges for all the little creatures."

"What a fine Christmas present for them all!" Sir David remarked.

"By splitting the thin trunks of young trees, then bending and tying them down and across, it can make a hedge grow thick and strong. It's called 'steeping' here in Devon, but old Radish, who has his own special names for everything, calls it 'uprightenin'."

"That's a very funny name for it," laughed
Sir David.

"I must remember that one. I can imagine how
happy all the little creatures must have been."

As they were so busy chatting and laughing, Lady Davina decided to go up to bed. Lord Peregrine saw her passing and called out to her saying, "I shan't be far behind you, my dear."

She loved this time of year as much as the youngsters. Lady Davina had never lost the feelings of excitement and wonder, or the thrill of waking up on Christmas morning.

Her own parents had always made her Christmas feel really magical and filled with love.

And so it was that, just as she had done ever since she was very young, Lady Davina once more made her special wish to Father Christmas.

At midnight the church bells rang out joyously into the cold night air, and Lady Davina drifted off to sleep.

It seemed only a few minutes later when she was woken by the sound of bells once again.

She sat up in bed and listened even more carefully – and there it was again, definitely the sound of bells. But they were not the deep rich tone of the church bells. These bells were tinkling, and sounded very tiny indeed.

Lady Davina went to the window and peered out. The sky was as dark as deep blue velvet, and the full moon shone softly down upon the silent gardens of the Manor House.

"What's the matter?" said Lord Peregrine sleepily from the depths of his pillows.

"Nothing dear," Lady Davina said softly. "Go back to sleep."

Suddenly Lady Davina saw something in the sky.

Silhouetted against its bright light, a miniature sleigh pulled by eight tiny reindeer flew in front of the moon, circling towards the Manor House.

"Am I dreaming?" she asked herself. Then she heard the bells again, and as she watched, she saw the sleigh land gently on the roof beside one of the large chimneys. At that moment she absolutely knew.

"Those are jingle bells!" she gasped.

To her amazement, a rather tubby and jolly looking figure dressed in red hopped out of the sleigh, lifted out a large sack and tossed it over one shoulder onto his back.

Lady Davina thought she heard a jovial "Ho ho ho!" before he disappeared down the chimney.

"What a good thing that Jeremy Jackdaw had swept each of the chimneys," she suddenly thought, imagining all the black soot.

"I knew it was true," whispered Lady Davina to herself. "Father Christmas, the sleigh, the reindeer… everything!" She climbed happily back into bed knowing they would all find their stockings full by the morning.

As she fell asleep, she thought about the one thing she would have most liked for Christmas. But as she had never told anyone about her secret wish, how could it ever turn out to be one of her presents?

Early next morning, the family gathered around the Christmas tree to open their presents amidst the wonderful smells of Christmas cooking that were wafting temptingly around the house.

Everyone was busy opening their parcels. Paper and ribbon flew everywhere.

Lord Peregrine and Lady Davina loved to watch the youngsters' faces. They always left their own presents until last, not wanting to miss a single thing.

Then Lady Davina spied a tiny parcel hidden amongst the branches of the Christmas tree.

She was amazed to see her name neatly written on its label.

Opening it carefully, she found a shiny, golden bell attached to a red silk ribbon.

Lady Davina gasped with delight and surprise. "It's just what I've always wanted!" she said. "A real sleigh bell."

"Who gave that to you?" asked Lord Peregrine, peering over his monocle. "It certainly wasn't me!"

"I expect it was one of the youngsters, dear," she said. "Anyway, it doesn't matter where it came from. It's just lovely."

Miranda and the twins were so busy playing with their new toys that they had not noticed Lady Davina's rather special gift.

But Lady Davina smiled to herself, as only she knew who had given her the beautiful sleigh bell…

...do you?

MERRY CHRISTMAS!

THE END
(...but the beginning of another exciting
New Year at the Manor House.)

How to Make Delia Duck's Starlight Biscuit Christmas Tree Decorations

Delia Ducks's Helpful Hints

Delia Duck says, "Before you start cooking, always wash your hands, put on an apron (just like Delia Duck!) wipe the surface where you will be working, get out all the ingredients and equipment and turn on the oven."

Remember ovens are hot, knives and cutters are sharp and it would be a shame to spoil your fun by having an accident, so always ask a grown-up to help you.

Now let's begin

On a table lay out 215g/8oz plain flour, 1 teaspoon baking powder, a small pinch of salt, 140g/5oz unsalted butter, 115g/4oz soft light brown sugar, 1teaspoon cinnamon, ½ teaspoon freshly grated nutmeg and 1 egg yolk.

For the icing: 200g/7oz icing sugar,1 tablespoon lemon juice and 2-3 teaspoons water, edible silver balls (optional.)

Then follow these instructions carefully:

Preheat oven to 180C | gas mark 4 (it takes about 15 minutes) and line two large baking sheets with non-stick baking parchment.

Use a sieve to sift the flour, baking powder and salt into a large bowl. Using your fingertips, rub the butter into the flour mixture until it looks like fine breadcrumbs.

With a tablespoon, stir in the spices, then the egg yolk and mix well into a dough. Dust your hands with flour and roll out using a rolling pin and a board lightly dusted with flour. The dough should be the thickness of a digestive biscuit.

Press out the biscuits with a star-shaped cutter dipped in a little flour each time you use it; this will stop the dough sticking to the cutter.

Place them onto the baking sheets. Carefully make a hole in a point of each star using a wooden skewer. Bake for about 6 minutes until golden brown, then move them onto wire racks to cool completely.

In a small bowl add the lemon juice to the icing sugar and stir in the water a little at a time until the mixture is a thick cream. Spread a little icing on each biscuit with a knife and decorate with silver balls.

When the icing is set, thread thin gold cord or ribbon through the holes in the stars and hang on the Christmas Tree, out of reach of any greedy pets!